If You Give A Skeleton A 3D Printer...

Diary Of The Skeleton In The Pond

LIANA BROOKS

OTHER WORKS

ALL I WANT FOR CHRISTMAS

All I Want For Christmas Is A Reaper
All I Want For Christmas Is A Werewolf

FLEET OF MALIK

Bodies In Motion
Change of Momentum

HEROES AND VILLAINS

Even Villains Fall In Love
Even Villains Go To The Movies
Even Villains Have Interns
Even Villains Play The Hero (omnibus)
The Polar Terror

TIME AND SHADOWS
The Day Before
Convergence Point
Decoherence

SHORTER WORKS

Fey Lights
If You Give A Skeleton A 3D Printer…
Prime Sensations
Darkness and Good

Find other works by the author at www.lianabrooks.com.

If You Give A Skeleton A 3D Printer...

Diary Of The Skeleton In The Pond

LIANA BROOKS

AUSTRALIA

Print ISBN: 978-1-922434-43-2
eBook ISBN: 9798201673703

www.inkprintpress.com

National Library of Australia Cataloguing-in-Publication Data
Brooks, Liana (1983—)
If You Give A Skeleton A 3D Printer…
54 p.   cm.
ISBN: 978-1-922434-43-2
Inkprint Press, Canberra, Australia
1. Fiction—Fantasy—Paranormal 2. Fiction—Fantasy—
Humorous 3. Fiction—Mystery & Detective—Amateur Sleuth

Summary: A skeleton is forced to 3D print themselves a body in order to save their pond.

First print edition: October 2021
Cover design © Inkprint Press.

This book is for everyone who would walk through a graveyard at midnight.

ACKNOWLEDGEMENTS

For most books the acknowledgments section is a long list of people I need to thank. In this case, it's more of a list of people to blame for enabling this silliness. You know who you are. Thank you for everything you do.

CONTENTS

What The Skeleton Did In The Dark 9

If You Give A Skeleton A 3D Printer 13

A Skeleton Goes To City Hall 16

The Skeleton And The Cryptids 20

A Skeleton's Thoughts On Interior Design 22

Night Of The Naked Skeleton 25

The Skeleton Solves A Mystery 28

The Skeleton Makes A Move 32

The Skeleton Faces The Music 35

WHαT THE SKELETON DID IN THE DARK

I found the internet! So helpful!

It took three tries, but I broke into the local library at night, and I've been spending all my midnights researching 3D printing material that feels like skin. It's not great, but I think I can get the squish right.

Let's see... does Thingiverse have muscles?

No? Why not??

Oh, right, I'm the only immortal skeleton wandering around St Louis—or probably anywhere. How would I even know? How do you even start that conversation? "Hi, so... are you just an undying skeleton in a suit too?"

I don't see that going well.

Okay... 3D scans of muscles... Oddly enough, Google is less helpful here.

I'm probably on a watch list now.

I know, 3D scans of famous statues.

Ooo! Do I want to be David or Venus de Milo? Hmmm. What was I when I was alive? I was... alive.

Yup, remember that. I think I broke my leg once, pretty sure, there's a line there that I have to glue up sometimes. I had an actual brain once too, but I guess some things soak into the bones and some things don't.

Maybe I'll print one set of muscles from each?

...Did you know the David statue was 17 feet tall? I did not.

Venus is 6'8". Eat your heart out, Gwendoline Christie![1]

Okay... Now... Order the stretchable printing filament... I figure I can use the MacGregors' shed, it has electricity and Mister MacGregor hasn't used the workshop since he broke his hip two years ago.

Can I use wood glue on my new muscles or do I need to buy a special glue?

Is there bone glue?

...Would I be able to get bone glue at the vet's office?

I hate going to the hospital, it's always so awkward. I sat down once and wound up hanging in an office for a week before they wheeled me into a

---

[1] Gwen, if you read this, don't be mad. I love you. I watched you in *Game Of Thrones* through someone's window. Let's be shopping buddies!

(I'm not a creeper, it's just hard to get people to invite you inside when you're a skeleton that smells like decayed leaves at the bottom of the lake.)

corner where I could grab something and escape. I still have the eye-loop screw thingy in my head.

Speaking of which, a wig. I need a wig. And makeup. Apparently I'm a girl now.

Right. Do I need boobs?

No, the internet says my secondary sexual characteristics do not determine my gender. Good to know.

Wait, I'm Venus, I have boobs. Do I need a bra? ...I'm thinking no. Bras are expensive.

Okay... Muscles, super glue, 3D printer, wig, makeup... Clothes? Um... Yes. I probably need those. They probably won't let a naked person into the planning office, even if she looks like Venus de Milo (or Gwendoline Christie). Fine. Clothes.

What size am I?

Size zero! Ahahaha! I crack myself up.

I better buy more glue. HA.

There we go. In three weeks I will have a new fleshy mass over my bony self and I can march into the planning office and demand my pond be left alone. My pond will be saved and I can go back to reading whatever falls to the bottom and sneaking out on Halloween.

They're putting some new houses up across the road, I should go lay in the dirt with an arrowhead and see if I can get this area declared a piece of historic importance.

I wonder if they could do a DNA test to see what I was when I still had skin. That'd be a hoot.

Ah, humans. such fun. But, you know what they say: Si non unum, terrent eos![2]

---

[2] If you can't be one of them, terrify them.

If You Give A Skeleton A 3D Printer

Okay, slight set back. As it turns out... there are about 600 muscles in the human body and, if you print them in fused lumps, they don't actually move very well. At all.

I make a great Venus though.

So, I tried water balloons for arm muscles, but they looked pretty fake. So, bear with me: since I found out how to get into the MacGregors' place[3] I found a stack of those new VHS.

...Okay, Google says VHS is NOT considered new anymore. I missed that bit.

Okay, so... Where was I going with this?

Movies... Balloons... PUDDING!

I found a video where someone makes fake muscle mass with balloons filled with pudding. The Mac-

---

[3] Storm cellar door into the basement... I almost got caught but I hid behind the Halloween decorations.

Gregors haven't changed their grocery list since 1998, so I have an ample supply of pudding. I added tapioca to the balloons on my hips for the realistic, cellulite look.

I don't know, maybe I'm vain, but I snuck in to see myself in the MacGregors' downstairs mirror (the little one over the sink that shows half a skull) and I think I look very alive. Very, very colorful. The clown balloons tied into fun shapes of cows around my calves looked a little inauthentic, but I now have fleshy guns of pudding.

You can't see me, but picture me posing.

I look A-MAY-ZING for a skeleton who has been sleeping at the bottom of a pond for, apparently, over six decades.[4]

Gosh. Does that mean Missus MacGregor might be related to that little girl who nearly drowned back then? Maybe. It feels right though, you know? There's a symbiosis or, uh, synergy? Is that a word? There's a connection.

Which is why I think she won't mind me borrowing some of the clothes down here.

My Venus de Milo face finished printing, it's a little large for my skull and there's no nuance or expression, but I found a makeup tutorial. I am rocking what the... YouTube-ist? Er? Gremlin? YouTube moving picture star? Whatever, I am rocking what they call the 'Retro Eighties Glam Look', which

---

[4] I needed a good nap.

I feel is going to allow me to blend in perfectly with the locals.

I even printed a pet for my new purse:[5] I 3D printed a tardigrade in a squishy orange filament. I named him Milo.

Get it? Venus and Milo? Venus de Milo?

Oh, I crack myself up!

Oh…

Oh!

Hmmm.

My pudding leaked.

I need more duct tape.

---

[5] Missus MacGregor's old one that was claimed by spiders in a corner and reclaimed by me.

A Skeleton Goes To City Hall

You will never believe the levels of discrimination in this city![6]

I went down to city hall in a perfectly acceptable outfit. And, okay, I admit the winter coat was a bit out of season, as were the gloves. But I had to cover the balloons! And the duct tape! I can't just walk into city hall the way I am!

In my defense the bright, cherry red of the coat totally matched the lipstick on my Venus de Milo mask I printed. I thought my new face was stunning, with lime-green eyeshadow, highlighter on the cheeks, and a festive little cat sticker I found in the basement. That turned out to be from a holiday bag of kitty litter.

There is no way I didn't look very, very, mostly

---

[6] Unless you are more up to date on the news than I am. Woof, but the 21st century has been bad!

human. I am human! I'm just... you know... a human with less organic matter than some people. That doesn't mean the young man sitting at the security desk of the city call had any right to call me names.

He was barely fifty if he was a day, and rude! Just... rude!

I am very lovely woman. Sort of. You know. Possibly once a woman. Definitely now a skeleton. But I am still human! If you prick me, do I not bleed?

...Don't answer that.

The real problem, in retrospect, all things considered, was probably not my fashion sense.[7] I suspect... Um, this is so embarrassing...

I don't have a nose, okay? Let's not judge. I am a skeleton. I have bones. I have some bone-deep intelligence, if you will.

But fleshless immortality didn't come with a nose. I have no olfactory sense. So... *sigh and stare into the distance—this will be great for a TikTok* ...I didn't realize that the MacGregors used to have a cat. And apparently they don't have a sense of smell either.

In fact... Okay, I didn't want to think about this, because I'll be sad...[8] But I'm not sure the MacGregors are alive.

---

[7] Which is to die for. Thank you.

[8] How am I sad? I don't have glands. This-doesn't-compute dot g-j-g? gif? Jif? Wiggly picture? This Doesn't Compute Dot Wiggly Picture.

I noticed the lights turn out at the same time of day every day, and even though the living had daylight savings,[9] the MacGregors didn't change their schedule. The TV flipped on the other night and the power glitched[10] and the TV just stayed on.

I'm a little worried, to be honest.

But, no, because someone definitely came down to the cellar that one day.

Oh... OH MY IMMORTAL SOUL AND BONES! WHAT IF THAT WAS THE MURDERER???

Oh no! Oh no!

What if I let a MURDERER kill the MacGregors and the only reason they didn't kill me is because they thought I was Halloween decoration?

Oh no.

This is terrible.

I was so worried about my pond that I let poor, sweet Missus MacGregor, who I totally think was once Milly Strudel... No, not strudel...

Pancake? Cookie? Pie? Let me google names of pastries...

DANISH! I totally think Missus MacGregor used to be Milly Danish, the little girl who nearly drowned last century.

---

[9] Google-people complained about this.

[10] Not at all because of how many things I was running in the shed—I'm nearly ninety-five percent certain no one will think to blame me, so it's not my fault.

What is the point of being an immortal skeleton skulking at the bottom of ponds if I can't save the fragile, fleshy little humans who are my nearest and dearest neighbors?

Yes, the pond is important, but I have to go save the MacGregors first.

…No. I need to take off the coat and gloves with the organic stench of a long-dead cat first, and probably rinse off the pudding that's leaking too.

Then I need to save the MacGregors!

THE SKELETON AND THE CRYPTIDS

I think the MacGregors count as cryptids. Right? Because *I* believe they exist, but no one has ever seen them.

At least, no one I have ever talked to.

The people on r/Cryptozoology were very kind when I asked about this. They fully support my monster hunting. I *may* have left out a few key details—I'm a skeleton, the MacGregors are human,[11] technically I am the monster—but isn't there a little monster in all of us? Is not man the true monster?

Am I not a man?

Don't answer that.[12]

The relevant bit of information is that, tonight, I am going to go into the MacGregors' house and look for them. I'm leaving my 3D-printed body and pud-

---

[11] Probably.

[12] Unless you know how I identified before I died. I sure as heck don't recall.

ding in the shed. If I get caught, I will collapse on the ground like a pile of bones and people will say, "Oh! How funny! I don't remember leaving a pile of bones there!"

People are always leaving piles of bones around the house. It could happen to anyone.

Besides, the MacGregors are old and have terrible eyesight. They'll probably think I'm their cat. …Who is also dead.

You know, on second thought, it's probably best if I don't get caught. I'll wear a blanket. That way, if someone sees me, I can fall down and they will see a blanket.

There's nothing less suspicious than a blanket.

A Skeleton's Thoughts on Interior Design

I miss mid-century modern decor. The orange shag carpets. Those funky, lime-green curtains that always smelled so slightly of mildew. Churning your own butter.

Wait...

...Was freshly churned butter mid-this-century or mid-last-century?

What century is it?

To the Google!

UPDATE: Shag carpet was mid-last-century and churning butter by hand was mid-the-century-before-that. Also, Americans eat an alarming amount of butter every year. I found a recipe for deep-fried butter that is said to be good with deep-fried coke.[13]

No, not the 1800's coke. The bottled caramel-fizzy water stuff.

Deep. Fried. Butter.[14]

---

[13] Texas… I have questions.

[14] So. Many. Questions.

I may need to just go back to the pond....

...No! No.

I will save the MacGregors first, then save my pond, *then* go back to my pond and forget everything Texas has ever deep-fried.[15]

Where was I?

Oh, yes, the house.

I went in through the doggy door. Why do the MacGregors have a doggy door? They've never had a dog. But they have a doggy door. Maybe for the late cat. I went in and found the kitchen quite clean. A bit dusty, with ants around the food in the mousetrap, but clean otherwise.

The house is decorated in a very regrettable early twenty-first century style, with blue-and-white chevron rugs and a self-painted chalkboard wall. I get that there was a recession, but did an entire living room wall need to be sacrificed as a chalkboard?

It's an accent wall in BLACK.

I'm as gothic as the next skeleton, but there really must be limits.

Missus. MacGregor needs autumn tones to complement her complexion. Black looks ghastly with her skin. It adds ten years.

I can only assume the grandkids are worth the interior design havoc.

---

[15] What is it about Texans and state fairs that bring out their worst culinary impulses?

The upstairs was probably the original late-90's paint. Beige and tan with touches of rose.

The guest bedroom is cluttered. I think I remember hearing something about a grandson staying with them? I think he's the one who got them into watching *Game of Thrones* in season three. But really I only remember the Red Wedding.

No MacGregors, though. Of any generation.

The beds were empty. There was no corpse floating in the tub. No skeletons in the closets. Well, not until I showed up at any rate.

It's perplexing. Vexing, even.

The phone works.

The electricity works.

The TV... Oooo! The MacGregors have a Hulu subscription! I'm going to watch *Game of Thrones* again.

Night Of The Naked Skeleton

Picture this—if you're brave—I'm sitting there watching Daenerys take control of the Unsullied, a knitted brown-and-orange afghan over my head as the morning light creeps in AND THE FRONT DOOR OPENS.

IT. OPENED.

Just like that!

No knock! No nothing! And all these voices start coming in.

I'm sitting there, naked as the day I first lost my flesh, and people walked in!

Oh! The embarrassment! Caught without my pudding!

I would have blushed if I still had blood.

Instead, I collapsed.

It was quick thinking on my part. I leapt to the side of the couch next to the wall like an agile, skinny cheetah and dropped with the afghan over me. I was like Batman, or some super skinny, super smart, super fast superhero.

The Flash!

I was The Flash!

And I didn't even flash my breast bones at anybody.

Ha!

I crack myself up.

The only tiny, teensy tiny oversight in my genius was that, in my haste, I may have left the TV on and a small MacGregor walked in while a man was being burned alive by a dragon.

This is fine.

The child goes a school where they have active-shooter drills. Dragons burning people alive can't be scary to a kid who has been trained to take down a grown man with an AR-15 since pre-school.

…

…

Let's move on.[16]

I have good news!

---

[16] I can only assume that it's too soon to talk about gun control laws, so let's talk about Dragon Control Laws. Should you be allowed to own a dragon? I think it's my Constitutional right as a skeleton to have a dragon. When is Congress going to give me my dragon?

The MacGregors have been spotted! The r/Cryptozoology people are going to be so excited that I had a successful cryptid hunt!

In fact, I will be able to add the news that the MacGregors have grown an extra set of ears while they were away. Is it a radiation-driven mutation because of polluted water? Did aliens take the family away? Is it a secret government experiment?

Oh! Look at that kid's cute Minnie Mouse dress. Adorbs.

...I think they went to Disneyland without me.

The Skeleton Solves a Mystery

THE MACGREGORS DID IT!!!!

Here I am worrying myself to death.[17] Worrying until I'm nothing but skin and bone.[18] Acting like a mad thing,[19] because I was worried about saving my dearly beloved pond from ruination AND THE MACGREGORS WERE THE ONES PLANNING TO DRAIN IT!!!

I feel utterly, utterly betrayed.

Haven't I always been there for them? Standing just outside their window? Watching the TV from the bushes?

---

[17] Obviously not Death-death, but you know. Death-*ish* worry.

[18] ...Okay, just bone. Which I started as. Bad analogy.

[19] Don't you even think about making the smart comment here.

Wasn't I always there when they needed a cup of sugar or a friendly ear? I didn't have either sugar or ears,[20] but that's not my fault! I'm not responsible for being a skeleton! I didn't make myself this way! ...That I know of.[21]

I'm off track... Where was I?

Oh!

Right!

I was hidden under an afghan next to the beige couch of the vile betrayers in their Mouse-y shirts. MacGregor The Elder was talking about how his hips weren't the same as they used to be. I sympathize. I'm fairly certain my hips aren't how they used to be either. Then MacGregor The Younger says not to worry, the building plan for the new house will have a ramp out front and no stairs inside.

Let me tell you, I very nearly gasped.

In part because MacGregor The Youngest was trying to pull my toes out from under the couch, but mostly because I was so broken up by the idea of the MacGregors leaving. They've been like family to me! Slightly distant, estranged, possibly judgmental family. But still family.

When the younger Missus MacGregor said she was going to turn the shed into a She-Shed, I pan-

---

[20] Ears are cartilage and they just don't last after the first few years of decomposition.

[21] I really need to look into that some day.

icked. That's my work room! My printer is there! My *body* is there.

Decent people don't just make you move your body without warning! Who do they think they are? Land owners?

Well, yes, as a matter of fact. They do own the land. The stand of oak trees over on the other side of the fence. Several acres of fallow farmland. And my pond.

As I sat there, fighting to keep my toes out of the mouth of Youngest MacGregor, I heard them talking about draining the pond. There was talk of back-filling, drainage sites, and pennycress.[22]

My precious, beloved, soggy, swampy, toad-filled pond is going to be drained and filled. My old tire that I spin around sometimes is there. And the broken chair where I sit when I get tired of laying in the mud. And there's the fender of the old car that I sometimes kick. And little, muddy golden shiners and fathead minnows. In the spring there's tadpoles and in the summer I have frogs in the pond.

What am I going to do?

Where am I going to go?

No home. No MacGregors' shed. No friendly neighbors letting me watch their TV through the window.

---

[22] Which I'm fairly certain is a villain in a Stephen King novel. I'm almost never wrong about these things.

I'm utterly bereft of everything that gave my life meaning.

I guess... I guess I'll have to pack my things. Move to the city. Find a crypt with some wifi or live under someone's porch.

It sounds very low class, if you ask me. Living under a porch like a snake instead of in a pond like a skeleton in a pond.

I've lost everything.

Including my shin bone.

Youngest MacGregor is banging it on the hideous chalkboard wall.

I'm going to cry.

The Skeleton Makes a Move

For those keeping score at home, your second-favorite skeleton[23] is not racking up the wins. But like a poolhall hustler, I'm going to come swinging back at the last second.

Milo, my bright orange tardigrade, and I are currently in the not-a-she-shed redoing the makeup for my Venus mask. According to my google-fu, the hot new trend for the year is bright eyelids and darker lip stains. On YouTube I found a tutorial about how to look like a flamingo. Naturally.

The glitter makes me happy.

It's the only thing that does. I just... I can't imagine moving. I've lived here all my unlife!

Unlived here all my life?

Unlived here all my unlife?

Me + Pond = 5EVR[24]

---

[23] I assume your favorite is the bone-mecha your fleshy gray matter is currently riding in.

[24] Reminder To Self: Check the Google to see this

It's really unfair. I think the MacGregors would agree I've made an ideal neighbor. I don't make a mess. (Except in the shed.) I hardly ever steal anything. I haven't once dented the wall. (That was Youngest MacGregor with my shin bone. I have chalk paint connected my fibula, thank you very much, Smallest MacGregor.)

And I realize that having MacGregor: The Next Generation move into the main house is practical. The Original Series MacGregors aren't young anymore and, while they don't need to be put out to pasture, I can understand why, maybe, they want to move things around. And, it's true, the south field does flood something wicked in the spring. It's made sense to move the drainage pond down there since the early eighties. Maybe eighteen eighties? I don't remember which century. I just remember my pond was built for Old Miss Lilly's ducks. So maybe seventeen eighty?

I need to go look up the history of St. Louis.

And figure out how to pack up my 3D printer stuff.

Do you think I can rent a car? I'm definitely over twenty-five. But I don't have insurance. And this doesn't seem like a thing fifteen minutes with GEICO[25] will fix.

------

is how to spell the unword correctly.

[25] GEICO Insurance: "Fifteen minutes could save you fifteen percent or more!"

Maybe I should go back to city hall. I could probably pass a driver's test. I have great situational awareness. Like, eyes on the back of my head. I have cat-like reflexes. I can see things out of the corner of my eye socket. It's just like... wow! And pow! And did you see that!

Like, if I spin around right now I'll see everything and remember. Watch!

Woosh!

Skeleton spins and what did I see? The rake by the open door. It's red—the rake not the door. The potting soil is knocked over. Missus MacGregor is staring at me. Milo's purse is next to the window. There are three spiders in the window.

I'm not scared of spiders.

At all.

Spiders are scared of me.

Not everyone can say that.

Wait... Something is off.

See? That's my Spidey Sense. My acute observational skills.

I saw a rake, and an open door, and Miss... us... Mac... Gregor.. .by... the...

Uh-oh.

Um.

Oops?

The Skeleton Faces The Music

Where to start...

Where to start...

Let's start with: I was right.

Missus MacGregor IS Milly Danish.[26] I was right and this is very important for you to know.

My conversation with Milly was a scream.

Literally. Her scream became more screams. Someone grabbed the old hunting rifle from the pantry. Moths were released. Moth-aggedon happened. People were yelling at each other. And the toddler started chasing me in circles.

It was a very confusing time for all of us.

After a bit the toddler got fussy and Mister MacGregor told me to stop moving or he'd get a sledgehammer. I'm not sure where from, there's no sledge-

---

[26] Spelled with an E—Denish—but pronounced Danish.

hammer around here, but he sounded sincere so I let it go.

We sorted through all the obvious questions:

Was this a prank? No.

Was I one of Liam's friends? I don't think so.

Was I the grandchild who needed to eat more? Fairly certain that is also a no.

Where did I get the 3D printer? The internet.

Was I a scammer here to steal Ma and Pa MacGregor's life savings? No, Walt's Mouse got to them first.

What was I? A skeleton. Obviously.

Who was I? The Skeleton. Obviously.

We sat in the twilight hour on the back lawn that needed mowing, listening to the evening birds. If I could have cried, I think I might have. They were draining my pond. MY POND. The only home I've ever known.

It's not much, but it's mine.

Maybe in life I had more.

Maybe there was a time when the pond was a small, insignificant thing.

But that's the thing about having very little: every little piece matters. When you're poor, you count every penny. When you're sick, you count every pain-free moment. When you are depressed, you count every smile.

All I have at the end of the day is the pond.

It's not much, but it's a place where I can go where no one judges me. I don't need a mask. I don't need to hide under a blanket. I don't need to listen to people shout at me.

"The pond is going," Milly said.

I didn't answer because... why bother? The living didn't want to hear my thoughts.

"It leaks into the basement and it's ruining the foundation anyway," she continued.

"Pond could be moved," Mister MacGregor said.

The younger MacGregor boy clicked his tongue. "Seems to me that having a skeleton around could help."

I sat up straighter.

Milly nodded. "Pa, just think of what the papers would write about the hay rides and corn maze we're building if there was a real skeleton in there."

"Do you do hauntings?" the younger Missus Mac-Gregor asked.

"Sure?" I guessed. "I mean, I don't walk through walls or anything. But I can show up as myself?"

The MacGregor clan whispered to each other.

Milly clapped her hands. "Then it's settled. We'll build a new pond for the skeleton and it can keep the 3D printer. In exchange, the skeleton from the pond will show up and haunt the farm during the autumn hubbub."

And that's where the story ends.

We set up a bell system, and I picked out some

furniture to sink into the new pond.[27]

I helped Milly clean out the basement and bury the cat.

Youngest MacGregor calls me S'Kelly. I thought about learning to rap.

Next week the diggers are coming to build me a new pond, and the elder MacGregors are going to start work on their tiny retirement home.

So I guess....

I guess I saved the pond?

By being me?

I saved the day by telling people I wanted a place to exist.

That's kind of magical when you think about it.

And so am I.

---

[27] Because it will be used for certification SCUBA dives during the summer. I promised not to scare new divers and Young MacGregor promised to take me SCUBA diving next time the family drives to California.

ABOUT THE AUTHOR

LIANA BROOKS is not a skeleton. Well, she is, but she's a skeleton encased in a socially acceptable mass of muscle and skin. Plus she has organs. Sometimes they are even functional.

Liana lives somewhere in the United States with her husband and children. She is known for her space operas, including the *Fleet of Malik,* a series of connected sci-fi romances about rebuilding after a decades long war; the enemies-to-lovers superhero series, *Heroes and Villains*; and the *Time and Shadows* time travel murder mysteries.

She also writes paranormal holiday romances in the *All I Want For Christmas* series.

You can find out more about Liana at her website, www.lianabrooks.com.

MORE BY LIANA BROOKS

ALL I WANT FOR CHRISTMAS
IS A REAPER

THREE O'CLOCK ON A THURSDAY AFTER-noon in April, and I had an unplanned three-day weekend. In Chicago, my favorite city in the world. There were thunderheads gathering over Lake Michigan with the smell of rain in the air but, for now, downtown was a delightful playground of rushing cars, stressed commuters, and the bitter tears of lives I'd ruined with a pink slip.

With nowhere in particular to be, I meandered, crossing Clark Street at the light to reach a small city park with maple trees that wouldn't reach maturity in this century, a little playground with a sun shade, and a recycled rubber tire running track that crossed through the limited greenspace like a drunken snake trying to bite its own tail.

It was too early for school to be out and too late for lunch, which meant the park was populated by a muddy handful of toddlers, their attendant adults, and me. I kept to the outside track, crossing a stone footbridge over a shallow dirt ditch that might become a small pond if it rained. Tulips bobbed in the wind. The forsythia was out.

Little flowers and cheeky sparrows.

I enjoyed it for about four minutes before I could feel my brain scrabbling around like a trapped rat desperate for escape.

Natural vistas had that effect on me. I needed something to think about. A job to focus on. Numbers. Problems. City things.

At the sound of a jogger approaching, I stepped to the side so they could sweep past and catch the running track.

And sweep past he did. A gloriously muscular runner with olive-toned tan skin, a shock of silver-white hair shaved on the sides and long on top, a well-defined back and legs, and a black shirt sliding out of his waistband and dropping to the ground.

Well then.

It wasn't quite the young Miss Bennet dropping her gloves so a militia man could retrieve them for her, but it was possibly the twenty-first century equivalent. Even if it wasn't, it was only polite to collect the handsome man's shirt and return it to him.

I picked it up, shook off the dust and grass clippings, and held the sandalwood-scented shirt up for inspection. The owner was broad shouldered and the shirt was lean cut, meant to hug him and give everyone looking an excellent view of his well-defined muscles. Slightly more interesting was the word KILLER written across the front of the shirt in the font of the well-known horror brand, Slasher.

The jogger was a scary movie fan.

Not a lot to work with as openings went.

Scary movies weren't my cup of cocoa. No movies were, most days. Sitting still for hours on end listening to other people talk made me restless.

Perhaps it wasn't meant to be.

I folded the shirt neatly, and when I looked up the jogger was watching me from the bend of the running track only a few feet away, one white earbud hanging off his shoulder, the other still in his ear. He was younger than the white hair suggested, maybe twenties or early thirties, with dark brown—nearly black—eyes, high cheekbones, a well-defined jaw line, and a sharp, straight nose. He looked exceptionally intense and unquantifiably captivating.

"Is that my shirt?" he asked in a deep voice as delicious as he was. I could listen to that man read the dictionary and I'd love every moment of it.

I held the shirt up, letting it unfurl over my dress. "I don't know, do you think it's mine?" I let him get a good look at me. Large, dark reds curls that looked a century out of date, a pink flower tucked behind my ear, pink lipstick, pretty smile, A-line green dress with pink flowers embroidered on it and a crinoline underneath for volume; I looked like a piece of walking history.

Twee. Sweet. Friendly.

Stupid.

I'd heard every verdict, but the dress made me

look fabulous and I loved bringing a pop of cheer to people's otherwise blighted lives.

"It'd look good on you. Killer." The corner of his mouth lifted in a sexy smile.

Oh. No. I did not like that.

Actually, I did, very much, but I knew where sexy smiles led. It would be hot nightclubs, wild parties, and then a trip to the suburbs as Mr. Sexy waxed lyrical about 'getting away from the city.' Pretty soon he'd be browsing baby name websites and talking about getting a dog.

No. If a Timberwolf Town werewolf couldn't tempt me, then a yappy little dog suitable for the suburbs didn't stand a chance.

I held the shirt to my shoulders and tried not to notice how good it smelled—sandalwood with an undertone of mint. The scent was too light for a cologne—probably a soap. "It looks like my size, too." Assuming it was supposed to be worn halfway to my knees. Jogging, dark, and handsome was also tall, dark, and handsome.

"I'll let you borrow it some time." The man had dark, hungry eyes that promised to make my flirtation worth my time.

"Sure." That was never going to happen. I tossed the shirt to him. "Enjoy your run."

The smile turned to a smirk. "Enjoy the view." He secured the shirt to his waistband again and took off with a wink.

Confidence was always sexy, and I was very tempted to continue my little stroll around the park and see if the jogger wanted to join me for a post-workout snack somewhere.

I was great at first dates. Lots of confidence and a big smile got me everything I wanted.

Second dates?

No one had tempted me enough to schedule a second date since college.

I glanced at the jogger again. Maybe no one had tempted me?

He looked familiar in that we–met–once–in–passing sort of way.

My memory for names and faces was legendary, but I couldn't recall being introduced to him before.

It was going to bother me all afternoon if I didn't pursue it.

As if the office had a psychic link, my phone rang, the quick staccato tattoo reserved for my boss. Work was there again, to rescue me from my worst impulses and save me from the kind of heartbreak ice cream couldn't fix.

"Hi, Amara." I moved toward the crosswalk, dodging a little green car that nearly swerved into me. Chicago drivers. So charming.

There was a tiny community garden space across the street, a safe distance from the sexy jogger.

"Merri, I just heard the good word from Windy City Security, you've officially slayed the wicked witch of the upper west side. Did you break seven minutes?" Amara Rosa Park was just as competitive as I was and she'd had my back in the office betting pool.

Sloan and Markham is the name in corporate accounting in Illinois. Amara is the head of the forensic accounting unit.

Really, we're a bunch of math nerds who read too many mystery novels and decided we'd grow up to fight white collar crime for a six-figure annual salary. And in the land of the nerds, I'm the big, brutal boss, the final, unconquerable hurdle.

"Six minutes," I said with a killer smile.

"You make me so happy! Did Dulcie cry? I met her when I went in for the initial contact and..." Amara sighed. "Some people just look evil, you know?"

I pictured Dulcie Waterhouse in her gray pantsuit with a black silk shell under the jacket, two silver studs in each ear, a professional, asymmetrical cut for her dark brown hair, and dark red lipstick on a mouth pouring out more cuss words than could fit into a Monday morning commute when the trains were down. "She didn't cry, but you may need to give the interns a bonus for reading my emails for the next few weeks."

"More death threats?" Amara sighed again. "What is it about you that attracts so much venom?"

"It's the job." And the fact that dressing like the

lead singer from a retro throwback band made everyone underestimate me. What can I say? I have brains and beauty.

With a click of her tongue, Amara dismissed the disappointing news. "Well, done is done. I'll give the interns a heads up." There was a chime in the background. "Oh, and there's the first hit on social media. Want to hear it?"

"It's not like I'm going to look it up." I didn't do social media. Despite having an email assigned to me along with my social security number, I had the digital footprint of a ghost.

"The headline is 'Chicago's Infamous Grim Reaper Strikes Again.' Good job."

"I try my best."

Amara made a happy, purring sound. "Did you try your very best with Harry?"

"Harry?" I stopped in front of a bench. "I'm drawing a blank."

"Junior executive in accounting?" Amara dangled the tidbit.

Mentally I flipped through a detailed list of junior accounting people. "Not ringing any bells."

"Henderson account?"

I shuddered.

"He sent you a gorgeous bouquet of day lilies—"

"He was telling me about how his parents were building a new house in Sugar Grove and how the commute was under thirty minutes to the city with the new high-speed trains."

There was a stunned silence and then Amara took a deep breath. "So…"

"So, thanks but no thanks? Give them to someone else."

"He left a note too."

Stupid man. But it was only polite to read the note and find some excuse for why I couldn't show up to Domestication Of The Wild Wifey 101. "Leave it on my desk. I'll deal with it when I get back to the office."

"About that…."

"You have another job for me before the weekend?" If there were gods who smiled fondly on math nerds, I would have prayed. Numbers and patterns were my favorite candy. A weekend sorting through someone else's finances as just as blissful as a bubble bath.

There was a hesitant little sigh, which meant Amara wasn't sold on the job but someone was begging. "This is an odd one. It's not the bosses calling, it's an employee, and she asked for you by name because she said you worked here, but she didn't seem to know what it is you do."

Weird. "The name?"

"Ellen Berry."

Someone else would have a hazy memory of a schoolyard friend who they'd met during a game of tag–turned–head–on–collision in kindergarten. My memory was sharper than that, and off the top of my head I could rattle off all the major life events in Ellen's personal history up until she left for college in New York. We hadn't kept in touch mostly because I forgot people existed when I was working with math.

It was great for my bank account, but not for relationships.

"Merri?" Amara waited. "If I give you the address can you go over and see what's going on?"

"Sure. Where am I headed?"

"Cozy Studios—"

"Cozy as in Cozy TV with the candy-dipped romances?" Good grief. "Can I fire the writers for their poor plotlines?"

"Only if they're embezzling," Amara said. "Otherwise, give them the quick two-day special. A little workflow advice. A little hiring advice. And then get out of there, because we have the Oretega account to tackle next week."

Easy as mud pie in Mississippi. "Got it. In. Out. Tear-free."

"If you make it tear-free, I will personally buy you dinner anywhere in the city."

"I like expensive food," I warned.

"Cozy was just bought out by Slasher Corp," Amara reported with maybe just a soupçon of glee. "You're getting called in because Cozy is getting killed."

Keep reading!
Grab your copy now at:
<u>www.inkprintpress.com/lianabrooks/</u>
<u>christmas/reaper/</u>